HELPER AND HELPER

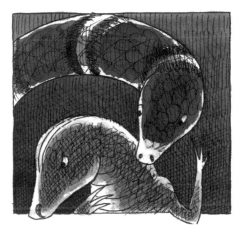

Snake and Lizard

Joy Cowley / Gavin Bishop

GECKO PRESS

This edition first published in 2017 by Gecko Press
PO Box 9335, Marion Square, Wellington 6141, New Zealand
info@geckopress.com

Distributed in the United States and Canada by Lerner Publishing Group,
www.lernerbooks.com
Distributed in the United Kingdom by Bounce Sales and Marketing,
www.bouncemarketing.co.uk
Distributed in Australia by Scholastic Australia, www.scholastic.com.au
Distributed in New Zealand by Upstart Distribution, www.upstartpress.co.nz

Gecko Press acknowledges the generous support of Creative New Zealand

ARTS COUNCIL OF NEW ZEALAND TOI AOTEAROA

Edited by Jane Parkin
Design and typesetting by Vida & Luke Kelly, New Zealand
Printed in China by Everbest Printing Co Ltd, an accredited ISO 14001 & FSC
certified printer

ISBN hardback: 978-1-776571-47-5
ISBN paperback: 978-1-776571-05-5
Ebook available

For more curiously good books, visit www.geckopress.com

For my beautiful granddaughter Aja Raue–
I am so proud of you

Contents

Democracy

The day was new, fresh and cool, scented with sagebrush. Although the desert still had shadow, the sun made a rim of fire on the top of Buzzard Mountain and the sky was slowly turning from grey to blue. Snake and Lizard sat outside their burrow, knowing that it was too late for owls and too early for Coyote, who sometimes came to them, pretending she needed help.

'You know what her problem is,' said Lizard. 'She's too stupid to know we see through her little schemes.' Pretending to be Coyote, he pointed to his mouth. 'Oh Snake! Oh Lizard! I have a sore tooth!'

Snake was amused. She and Lizard had been helping desert creatures for almost twenty-seven moons, and they knew there was only one thing on Coyote's mind. Food! They decided to make a few rules. Some creatures could not be helped, especially eagles, hawks and coyotes.

Snake slid into an early patch of sunlight. 'Lizard, my dear friend, it's time we had a meeting.'

Lizard looked puzzled. 'We meet every day, dear Snake.' Then his eyes widened. 'Oh! You mean a business meeting!'

'It is not a business, Lizard! We are Helpers, and helping is a profession.'

'Right! Exactly right, Snake! Profession sounds much better than business, only—'

'Only what?'

'If it's not business, why do we make our patients pay?'

Snake shook her head. 'Number one, Lizard, we don't make them pay. As professionals, we ask for a consultation fee. Number two, they are not patients.'

'You called them patients!' squeaked Lizard. 'You've always called them patients!'

'That was before I realised how impatient they were. All that pushing and shoving to be first in line. All that squeaking when we go into the burrow to have our supper. When did we last see a patient squirrel? Or rabbit!? No, we will call them clients.'

'All right. They're clients.' Lizard was cold and Snake

had taken the only close sunlight patch. 'Is that the end of our busin— our meeting?"

'Of course it isn't! We need to discuss a reception room. Do you remember how we worked together to take out the wall between our burrows?'

Lizard preferred to forget about that. His toe remained crooked after Snake had dropped a rock on it.

'We need a room inside our burrow, big enough for a rabbit. We can't talk to our larger clients outside. With Coyote and her mob sneaking about, it's extremely dangerous. It is also—' She looked for a word.

'Unbusinesslike?' suggested Lizard.

'Unprofessional,' said Snake. 'We can do it, Lizard! A fine reception room inside our entrance! It won't take more than a day to hollow it out. Do you agree?'

Lizard groaned at the thought but was anxious for an end to the conversation. 'I agree. Is that it?'

'How can it be?' Snake's tongue flickered. 'We have other concerns. You remember that great fuss of furious feathers about our sign?'

Lizard nodded. The mention of quail eggs as payment had become very embarrassing. Hundreds of small birds, their topknots fluttering with rage, had blocked the entrance to their burrow until Snake had to put a black line through the word quail on the notice board. There was, however, something else about the sign that bothered Lizard. Snake's name was always first. 'We should have a new sign,' he said.

'Exactly what I was thinking!' cried Snake. 'A huge sign at the entrance of our burrow! Snake and Lizard, Helper and Helper. Big help one egg. Little help one beetle.'

Lizard said in a small squeak, 'Lizard and Snake.'

'What?'

He lifted his chin in defiance. 'Lizard and Snake! Lizard and Snake!'

'My dear friend, we can't have that. Creatures are used to Snake and Lizard. They'll think Lizard and Snake is a new partnership.'

Snake was looking rather flustered and that gave Lizard courage. 'But it's my turn to go first on our sign!' he insisted. 'That's only fair!'

With a pretend laugh, Snake changed the subject. 'Look, Lizard! The sun is up and over the mountain.

That means there'll be blue flies down by the swamp. You need to go there, lickety-split, or you'll miss your breakfast. The rest of our meeting can wait until tomorrow.'

Lizard was cross. He humphed all the way down to the river, which had almost stopped flowing but was still rich with mud worms and flies. Not fair, not fair, he grumbled to himself. He was sick of bossy Snake telling him what to do. If she wanted her name first on their sign, he would take his name off. Snake could be a Helper on her own.

He didn't know if it was his anger or the sun that made him hot, but he was glad to wallow in the cooling mud. He was soon covered in a sticky brown coating that so changed his appearance, his twenty-third cousin, Green Lizard, didn't recognise him.

'I was good and mad,' Lizard explained. 'I needed to cool off.'

Green Lizard stood still to listen to the story.

Lizard knew his cousin didn't understand the helping business, but he needed to talk to someone. 'It's my turn to be number one on the sign outside our door!

She won't listen! I try to explain and she laughs at me.'

Green Lizard had turned his interest to the flies that were now rising in a thick cloud. He gulped down several before he said, 'You need to run your business along democratic lines.'

Democratic lines? What were they? Lizard wondered if they were marks in the earth.

His cousin said, 'You do know what a democracy is—don't you?'

'Sure I do!' said Lizard. 'I've known that for ages.' He tapped the side of his head with a claw. 'It's just that when I get upset, I forget things.'

Green Lizard stared at him for a long time and said slowly, 'Democracy is government by all creatures. It means everyone has equal rights. Tell that to your snake. Tell her if you don't have equal rights you'll go on strike.'

'Oh no!' Lizard was alarmed. 'She is very quick. She'd strike me first. She's not toxic but you should see her fangs! They're sharp as cactus thorns and I—'

'Stop!' His cousin leaned forward so that they were almost touching noses.

'Strike means you refuse to work. Got it? Going on strike is when you say goodbye and leave her to run the business on her own.'

'Is it? Oh yes!' Lizard smiled. 'Thanks, cousin! That's exactly what I was thinking. You just gave me some words for it, and I'm going back there to tell her face to face—'

But Green Lizard had moved away to the other side of the swamp.

Democracy! Democracy! As he ran to the burrow, Lizard said the word over and over so he wouldn't forget it. Democracy meant equal rights, and equal meant no one was better than anyone else. This glorious thought filled him with goodness and he called out a happy 'Hello, Friend!' to a tarantula spider that stared at him and then scuttled into a cleft in a rock. Democracy! It was a powerful word. Snake was clever. She would understand.

But when he arrived home, all the goodness rushed out of him in a loud squeak. No! Oh no! While he'd been away, Snake had made a new sign. On a large piece of bark, marked with a burnt stick, were the words:

It was too much for Lizard. His eyes bulged and his stomach shook with rage. He jumped up and down, shrieking, 'Not fair! Not fair!'

Snake slid close. 'Oh Lizard, what's wrong? I thought you'd like it.'

'You've done it again!' cried Lizard. 'It was my turn to be first!'

She tried to comfort him. 'I thought we'd discussed that.'

'No, we didn't. You sent me down to the creek so you could—could—'

He was too angry to finish the sentence.

'I really did think you'd like it,' she said. 'It was going to be a nice surprise.'

'It isn't nice! I told you—' Then Lizard remembered the special word. 'I want democracy!'

Snake swayed slightly. 'Democracy? Where on earth did you hear that?'

'Down by the creek. My twenty-third cousin, Green Lizard, explained it! Let me tell you what it means!'

'I know what it means.' Snake smiled gently. 'It's the way human things decide who's going to control their herd. It doesn't apply to us.'

Lizard knew Snake would try to change the subject. He said firmly, 'It's about equal rights.'

'Yes, yes,' she said soothingly. 'But some human things are more equal than others. They vote, you see, and just over half get the bosses they want. Just under half get the bosses they don't want. Democracy is not a very efficient way to manage a herd.'

Lizard was not going to be put off. 'I want my name first,' he said. 'It's my turn. I demand equal rights or I'll go on strike.'

Snake shivered, making it clear she knew the other meaning of 'strike'. He watched her uncoil and slither to the new sign. She said, 'Look at this! We are equal, dear Lizard. If your name was first we'd be unequal.'

'What?'

'Your name is longer. It has more letters than mine.'

Lizard counted. S-n-a-k-e. L-i-z-a-r-d. 'It's only one letter longer!'

'That's still bigger than mine,' said Snake. 'If you really want equality, I can do another sign and your name can be first. But we'll have to take off one letter.'

'That's ridiculous!' cried Lizard.

'Which do you prefer? Izard and Snake, or Lizar and Snake?'

He hopped up and down. 'You're trying to twist things! It's not fair!'

'On the contrary, my dear Lizard, I am trying to be very fair. It's all about being equal. Isn't that what you said?'

Lizard's stomach hurt but he didn't know if that was anger or because he hadn't had breakfast. Argument was useless. He turned his back on Snake and ran down to the swamp.

The sun was high and the desert shimmered with waves of heat. Most of the flies would be gone by now, but he might find a few mud worms. His feet skimmed over the hot earth. What was the word he'd tried to remember? Some of it came to him, and he muttered it over and over. 'Mockery, mockery, mockery!'

Payment

When Lizard came back from the swamp, he was still angry and hungry. Even worms had been in short supply. The footprints in the mud told him that ducks had been fossicking. He was full of self-pity, and the new sign next to the entrance of the burrow did not make him feel better. He wandered past it, settling under an old ocotillo bush where he would not be seen by soaring hawks.

Life was extremely unfair!

Snake came out to look for him. At first she thought she'd been clever, finding a way to keep her name first on the sign, but now Lizard was sulking, and if there was one thing Snake could not tolerate, it was a sulker. Especially her dear friend Lizard! His cheerful chatter could be annoying, but mostly it filled the empty spaces in her day and made her feel she was a good friend. Now she didn't feel like a good friend. She needed to do something about that.

She curved her way through the sparse undergrowth, the rustling dead leaves, and eventually found Lizard under his favourite ocotillo bush. He was pretending to be asleep, but she knew he wasn't, because his tail twitched.

'I've been thinking,' she said, and waited for him to open his eyes.

He didn't.

'There is something that is definitely not fair. Are you listening, Lizard dear? It concerns the helping payment.'

His eyes remained shut, but he said, 'Consultation fee.'

'Quite right. I stand corrected. You may have noticed that most of our clients pay with eggs. We both know why. Even if their problems are tiny, a mere half a beetle's worth, they still think they're big. So they bring the big payment.'

'Eggs,' muttered Lizard. 'For you.'

'I agree it's unfair.' Snake slid a little closer. 'I get eggs in great variety and number. Big eggs. Little eggs. All shapes and sizes. You get only a few beetles. Dear Lizard, the fee has been heavily in my favour.'

'Heavily,' Lizard echoed.

'I have decided, from now on, I'm going to share my consultation fee.'

Lizard opened one eye. 'I can't swallow eggs like you, Snake. I don't have an elastic mouth.'

'You can eat small eggs,' said Snake. 'Of course you can! Are you still hungry?' Lizard didn't answer, which meant yes, and she added, 'Wait here! I'll bring you four little eggs.'

Lizard was going to say, don't bother, because he

wanted to feel sorry for himself, but his stomach was almost empty and it was complaining. Yes, he could bite through small eggshells. He definitely could! He imagined breaking open four sparrow or quail eggs and sucking out the sweet yellow yolk. The more he thought about it, the more he understood that having his name first on the sign was not important compared with payment. No one could eat words.

He waited a long time with his eyes wide open, expecting to see Snake rolling four eggs towards him. But when she came, she was holding a leaf in her mouth. Carefully, she lowered the leaf to the ground. 'There!' she said. 'Delicious!'

It was a while before he realised there were four tiny balls on the leaf. They were white and they shone as though they were wet. 'What are they?' he asked.

Snake smiled. 'Spider's eggs,' she said.

The Healer

Snake hoped the new sign would attract more clients, but in fact the reverse happened. There were no new appointments.

'Don't worry,' said Lizard. 'It's the hot weather. Everyone's too tired to have problems.'

'We're not tired,' said Snake, 'and our problem is that desert creatures don't have any. If this continues, we'll have to go out and hunt for food. But I suppose we can look on the bright side. The lack of clients gives us time to create our new reception room. Oh, come on, Lizard! Don't pull a face! It will only take a day.'

Lizard groaned, knowing that the digging would take at least three days and he would be doing most of the work.

He was correct. It wasn't just the reception room that needed to be dug out. Having an area for bigger animals was useless unless they also enlarged the entranceway, and it was Lizard who had to do most of the scratching and much of the carrying of dirt. Snake was not well equipped for digging.

The most difficult areas were the ceilings, which had loose stones and clay and hanging roots. Showers of earth came down on Lizard's head, sometimes blinding him. Snake carried the stones out in her mouth, and when her mouth was empty, she told Lizard what to do. She did, however, keep him fed on woodpecker eggs and that was a welcome change from the taste of dry dirt. They finished towards the end of the third day.

The hollow that formed the reception room was big

enough for two squirrels plus both Snake and Lizard, and with a layer of dried leaves on the floor, it would be very comfortable.

Except that no one came. Not the next day, or the one after.

Grump Tortoise was the first to tell them why. 'Are you finding work a little quiet?' he called.

'Ignore him,' said Snake, who didn't like Grump Tortoise.

But the tortoise had a thick shell and would not be ignored. He came closer, dark eyes glinting with mischief. 'I hear you got yourselves some competition.'

Lizard did his best to make up for Snake's rudeness. He bounced forward, holding out his front paws. 'Hello Grump! We've got a brand-new reception room. If you need help, we'll show it to you.'

Grump Tortoise smiled. 'If I need help, I'll go to the new Healer—Doctor Grey Rabbit. Animals are lining up to see him. They say he can fix anything from fleas to fur drop.'

'Grey Rabbit?' Snake's mouth hung open.

Grump Tortoise smiled, his eyes disappearing in

wrinkles. 'I thought you would have known. He's the talk of the desert, old Doctor Grey. Animals are flocking to him. It's good to have someone who can really heal.'

With a deliberate chuckle, he lumbered away, leaving them bewildered.

More information came from a twittering hummingbird who could not stay still long enough to answer questions. 'Yes. Yes. Rabbit. Grey. Healer. Famous. Bye.'

Gradually, other desert dwellers filled the gaps in their knowledge. Grey Rabbit was one of the jackrabbit

clan living on the foothills of Buzzard Mountain.

Until recently, he was known only for his quick temper. It came as a surprise to Snake and Lizard that he had set himself up as a Grand Healer, claiming special powers from the sun.

'It's true!' gabbled a squirrel. 'Doctor Rabbit's body changes sunbeams into healing energy that comes out through his paws.'

'What nonsense!' said Snake. 'If you believe that, you'd believe anything.'

The squirrel sniffed. 'You're jealous because he's better than you.'

'I am not jealous!' Snake said in a cold voice. 'Lizard and I are Helpers, not healers, and we don't make ridiculous claims for ourselves. Huh! If he's a doctor, I'm a centipede!'

'You don't heal,' said the squirrel. 'You just talk. What use is that?'

Snake stretched up until she was taller than the squirrel. 'We do what we can,' she said.

'And sometimes we do what we can't,' added Lizard.

With Snake towering over her, the squirrel decided

it was time to leave. When she had gone, Snake and Lizard had a serious discussion about real Helpers, fake healers, unreliable clients, eggs and beetles.

'Our reputation is at stake,' said Snake.

'We'll go bust,' said Lizard.

The situation was serious, and they both knew that an angry reaction could make it worse. The sensible thing was to visit Grey Rabbit and point out that they were actually partners. There was a difference between helping and healing. Snake said to Lizard, 'If he truly has a long line of animals at his door, he won't be able to cope. He can sort them into two groups. Those that need help can come to us.'

'Snake, you are so wise,' said Lizard. 'That will solve his problem of too many and our problem of too few.' He corrected himself. 'Our problem of none.'

'I'm glad you agree,' she replied.

Away they went, side by side, Lizard walking, Snake slithering. When they went out together, as on this day, they combined the words and described the journey as a wither. It was indeed a very long wither to the hill where Grey Rabbit lived with the rabbit hordes. But once they got there, it was easy to find him. The reports were correct. A long line of small animals jostled and squeaked outside his burrow. As Lizard and Snake withered to the front of the line, there were unhappy mutterings and shouts of 'Wait your turn!', but the Helpers went on until they were facing the old Doctor Rabbit himself. He was sitting on a stone covered with desert marigolds and, on each side, a rabbit waved a fan of sagebrush to keep him cool. Snake thought he looked ridiculous.

'What do you want?' Grey Rabbit demanded.

His voice was so sharp, Lizard jumped and even Snake quivered, although she pretended she was simply shrugging off some dust. She raised her head and said, 'Good afternoon, Grey Rabbit. May we have a moment of your time?'

The old rabbit stood up to make himself taller. 'Doctor Grey Rabbit, if you please, and no, you may not have my time. I have patients waiting. Go away!'

Snake kept her voice calm. 'Yes, you have many patients. Too many, perhaps. Lizard and I have an idea that could help you—'

'Go away!' he shrieked. 'I know you two. You're not Helpers! You're useless!'

Snake raised her voice. 'You can at least be polite. We are offering you a valuable service, and you call us names. That is not very professional!'

'You are very bad-mannered!' shouted Lizard.

Doctor Grey Rabbit's anger exploded into fury. His eyes bulged. He leapt up, knocking over the young rabbits who were trying to fan him. 'I'll call down the sun and scorch you with my paws!' he screamed. 'I'll turn you into ashes.'

His voice was so loud that some of the animals came forward to growl and hiss at Snake. A kangaroo rat showed his teeth, and a porcupine raised her quills to resemble a forest of thorns.

Lizard nudged Snake. 'Let's go!'

They had no choice. They withered with sensible speed down the slope of the hill.

Back at the burrow, Lizard asked, 'Could he really have done that?'

'Done what?'

'Called down the sun? Burned us with his paws?'

Snake snorted. 'Of course not, Lizard! Creatures say things like that when they want to appear powerful.'

Lizard wasn't so sure. 'Maybe it was true,' he said. 'Those little rabbits were trying to keep him cool.'

'Lizard dear.' Snake put her head against his. 'You are not the sharpest thorn on the cactus, but even you know the difference between hot sun and a hot temper. The only thing they have in common is they come and go. When that stupid rabbit has time to think, he will turn up at our door, asking for help.'

'Are you sure?' Lizard looked anxious.

'Positive,' said Snake. 'He's old. He can't manage that lot on his own.'

But it wasn't Doctor Rabbit who came to their burrow the next day. The hissing, clicking sound was terrifyingly close. They had heard it many times in the distance and had shivered with fear. Now it sounded like an avalanche of little stones. It was the voice of death and it was at their door.

'Help!' it called. 'Are you in? I need help!'

In their worst fears, they had never imagined this situation. It was worse than one of the owls, worse than Coyote. They had a turkey vulture for a client.

They crept into the new reception room and looked through the tunnel to the entrance. Even Snake, whose sight was poor, could see the huge scaly feet fitted with sharp claws. The smell of the bird was overpowering. Its dusty feathers were soaked in the stench of decay.

The turkey vulture must have sensed them there, because she bent over until her bald head was on the ground by her feet. A red-rimmed eye stared into the burrow.

Neither Snake nor Lizard had seen a vulture this close before. The head was red and wrinkled skin, the beak strong enough to cut them in half with one snap. The round eye blinked. There was another hiss, a click, and the giant bird said, 'You're the Helpers, aren't you?'

'Yes.' Lizard's voice was a tiny squeak.

Snake added quickly, 'But our office is closed today.'

'I need your help,' said the vulture. 'I can't fly.' There was a rustle of black feathers, and a wave of bad smell came down the burrow. 'I can't get off the ground.'

Lizard whispered to Snake, 'What can we do?'

Snake murmured back, 'Have you got any ideas?'

Lizard shook his head. 'If she stays here, we can't go out. We have to do something.'

'Are you listening?' growled the vulture. 'I need help real bad.'

Snake raised her head a little and called, 'Do you have a broken wing?'

'No,' the vulture replied. 'Both wings are fine but I can't fly.'

'Are you scared of heights?'

Again the vulture said no. 'I told you, my wings won't lift me off the ground.'

Lizard whispered to Snake, 'Ask if she's had a big meal!'

Snake called, 'What have you eaten recently?'

'The carcass of a deer,' the vulture replied.

At this, Lizard became excited. He patted Snake's back. 'Tell her she needs help from a doctor!'

'What?'

'Tell her to go to Doctor Rabbit!'

Snake turned. 'Lizard, you are astonishing!' Then she called to the vulture, 'We'd like to help, but we take care of emotional problems. I'm afraid this is a serious medical problem You need to see Doctor Grey Rabbit who lives on the hill. He'll be able to treat you.'

'The old rabbit?' the vulture asked. 'Is he any good?'

Snake wanted to say, no, he's stringy and tough, but instead she carefully explained that Doctor Grey Rabbit had the reputation of being a great healer. 'There is always a long line of patients outside his burrow.' She smiled. 'You'll probably have to wait all day.'

When the vulture waddled away, Snake nudged Lizard, who hugged her.

They could not control their laughter. 'Imagine it!' gasped Lizard. 'A huge turkey vulture joining that line!'

Snake quivered. 'I wish we could see it.'

'All we have to do is wait for the result,' said Lizard.

That afternoon, a line began forming outside their burrow—squirrels, rats and mice, lizards, a couple of scorpions, a rabbit who was scared of the dark, even the grumpy porcupine. They'd all come down from the hill, and they all needed help. Snake and Lizard

worked until dark. The new reception room was full of clients and mounds of eggs and beetles.

The eggs were fresh, but the Helpers were too tired to eat. When the last client left, they lay on the dried leaves, exhausted.

Snake said, 'I wish I could have seen the panic. They say even Doctor Rabbit disappeared into his burrow. But I feel sorry for the vulture. That long walk for nothing!'

'No, Snake! Don't feel sorry for her. We helped her.

She had eaten too much to fly. A good long walk was what she needed. I'm sure she got off the ground.'

Snake chuckled. 'I don't think many of our clients will be going back to Doctor Rabbit. Who wants a healer that attracts vultures? That was your suggestion, Lizard. Where did you get such a brilliant thought?'

'From you, Snake.'

'Oh! Really?' Snake was pleased. 'Thank you, Lizard. I'm glad you sometimes listen to my advice.'

Lizard shrugged. 'It wasn't what you said, Snake. It was what you did. Long ago we went to that human thing's chicken farm. You swallowed nine chicken eggs.'

'Surely not!' said Snake.

'Yes, you did.'

Snake turned away. 'I'm sure you're mistaken.'

'I'm not,' said Lizard. 'You were so full you couldn't slither for three days.'

'I never did such a thing!' said Snake, and she went to the back of the burrow, where she couldn't hear him.

A Personal Name

Snake and Lizard had a steady number of clients. Some of them said they had left Doctor Grey Rabbit because they would not go to anyone who treated vultures, but it was obvious the old rabbit was still seeing a few patients. It didn't concern Helper and Helper. They had all the work they needed.

Local talk, now, was about a new rabbit who had escaped from the town and come to their part of the desert. At first glance he didn't look like a rabbit. He had white fur as soft as duckling down, pale eyes, a pale nose, and floppy white ears that hung down to his shoulders.

'That,' Snake said to Lizard, 'is what happens when animals live with human things. They lose all their colour.'

The white rabbit had found a home with a family of regular brown jackrabbits in a burrow by the old Joshua tree.

One morning when Snake was out, the white rabbit came to Lizard, asking for small help. Being larger than a brown rabbit, he needed to squeeze himself into the consultation room and, in doing so, he accidentally swallowed a dead beetle he'd been carrying in his mouth.

'I'm so sorry,' he said. 'I lost your fee. I'll get you another.'

Lizard was not accustomed to such politeness. 'Don't worry about it. I'm very happy to meet you. I am Lizard.'

'Well, thank you, Mr Lizard.' The white rabbit smiled,

showing two long front teeth. 'You are very kind. I am Fluffy. May I call you by your personal name?'

'Certainly,' said Lizard. 'Tell me, is it true that you escaped from a den of human things?'

'Yes, it is true. I was a pet kept in a cage, but one day the children left the door open. I must say the freedom of the desert is wonderful. The wild rabbits have been very kind, although I confess I feel rather nervous. My little problem is my colour.'

'You are white,' said Lizard.

'Precisely. I am very easily seen. I don't wish to criticise this beautiful desert, but I have noticed there are a few—some—well, one or two dangers.'

'Horned owls,' said Lizard. 'Hawks, vultures, bobcats, coyotes.'

The white rabbit shivered. 'You understand perfectly. Can you help me, Mr Lizard?'

'That's why I'm here,' said Lizard. 'I'm a Helper. Did you say your name was Fluffy?'

'That's correct. And your name?'

'You just said it. Lizard.'

'No, I mean your personal name.'

'My personal name?' Lizard didn't understand. 'That's it. Lizard.'

Now it was the rabbit who looked puzzled. 'What is your first name? The name that says who you are?'

Lizard said very slowly, 'I—am—a—lizard.'

The white rabbit's nose twitched. 'No, no! That's WHAT you are. It's not WHO you are. As well as Lizard you must have a name that makes you different from your brothers and sisters.'

Now Lizard understood. 'You mean my number! I'm thirty-seventh in my family. But no one calls me Number 37. I'm just Lizard.'

Fluffy Rabbit's ears drooped further and he said in a soft voice, 'The rabbits have numbers, too. It must be very boring to be known by a number. Human things all have first names that say who they are, and they give first names to their pets. They called me Fluffy. The cat was Whiskers and the dog was Patch. I think'—the pale nose twitched again—'I would feel sad if my name was only Rabbit. It's my first name that makes me feel special.'

'Oh,' said Lizard. 'That is very interesting.'

Long after the fluffy white rabbit had squeezed out of the burrow, Snake came slithering back, and Lizard told her about first names. 'Why don't we have names that describe us?'

'We do have an extra name,' Snake replied. 'It comes last. I am Snake Helper. You are Lizard Helper.'

'I didn't mean that! Helper is a business—I mean a professional title. I'd like a first name that said something about me—who I really am. What do you suggest?'

Snake yawned. 'You have a habit of jumping up and down. How about Jittery Lizard?'

'No,' cried Lizard. 'I'd hate that!'

'And you squeal a lot,' said Snake. 'I could call you Squeaker. Or Jabberer. How about something exotic like Hysterical?'

Lizard shook with anger. 'You are deliberately being horrible!'

Snake laughed. 'No! I was teasing you. Oh Lizard, can't you take a joke?'

'I'll call you Belly-Crawler!' shouted Lizard. 'Dirt-Slider! Frog-Eater! Egg-Thief.' He would have said

40

more but could not think of words bad enough.

The length of Snake's body quivered with laughter. Then she said, 'Oh Lizard! We don't need extra names. We know who we are.'

Lizard's temper fizzled out. He closed his mouth. It was true. They did know who they were.

Then Snake said, 'You haven't told me how you helped Fluffy White Rabbit.'

'I told him to go down to the swamp and roll in the mud,' Lizard said. 'That way he will be the same colour as the other rabbits.'

'Good advice, Lizard,' Snake said. 'But now he'll have to change his name, won't he?'

Lizard was quiet for a moment, then he said, 'I've been thinking—another name I could call you is Clever Snake.'

'And I could call you Kind Lizard,' said Snake. 'Now let's have some supper.'

Food and Friends

It was the dry season and the river was shrinking. It became a stream, then a swamp and then a series of muddy patches with a dry gulch between. Lizard had to go further to find the damp spots where there were still flies to be had. The flies were fewer and the competition had increased. Every fly-eating creature was there, pushing and shoving in the mud. Some of Lizard's cousins had no thought for family loyalty. They bumped him aside as though he were a dead leaf. The larger lizards reached over him to snatch a fat blue fly from his waiting mouth. Breakfast had become so difficult, he decided to change his feeding time. He would go to the pond at early light, before the flies became active. 'First come, first served,' he said to Snake.

'Lizard, you get wiser every day,' she said, and that pleased him. Snake didn't give compliments often.

But Lizard was not the only creature to arrive early. A brown frog with golden eyes was also there for a meal. He was a small frog and he knew a lot about river insects. 'The blue flies are big, but the sweetest are the little black flies in the reeds. Follow me. The black flies are still asleep on the stalks, and you can pick them off with your tongue.'

Lizard came home before sun-up, his stomach full. He couldn't wait to tell Snake about his new friend. 'He was very helpful! Not your usual frog with its nose in the air. We hunted in the reeds for those sweet little black flies.'

Snake yawned. 'Really?'

'Yes! You know those black ones that fly too high to catch? Before sunrise, they're still asleep on the stems. Slurp! Slurp!' Lizard patted his stomach. 'Oh Snake! I've had such a good breakfast!'

The next morning, as the sky in the east turned pale, Lizard scampered across the desert and down to the pond. Sure enough, the brown frog was there waiting. 'Black flies again?' he asked.

'Definitely,' said Lizard, and together they crept into the reeds.

The flies were small, and in the faint light looked like tiny black buds on the stalks. They didn't wake up, didn't try to escape, as Lizard's tongue flicked out.

There were so many of them! What a feast! He crawled between the clumps of reeds, cleaning one stalk after another until he couldn't eat another black lump. He called to the brown frog, 'Another delicious breakfast! Thank you, my friend.'

There was no reply.

He called again, louder this time. 'Excuse me! Brown Frog, are you there?'

After a few seconds there was a rustle in the reeds opposite. He ran across the mud patch and thrust his head between the stalks. 'Brown Frog?'

It wasn't the brown frog. It was Snake.

Lizard stared at her. 'What are you doing here?'

Snake didn't look at him. 'Same as you,' she said.

A bad feeling came over Lizard. 'You don't eat black flies! You don't like any flies!'

Snake didn't answer but slid away from the pond. As Lizard ran after her, he couldn't help but notice a small bulge in her body. 'You ate Brown Frog!' he shrieked.

The sun was now making long morning shadows across the desert, and creatures were running on their way to the ponds. Lizard ran in the opposite direction, trying to keep up with Snake. 'You ate my friend! You did! You ate him!'

Snake stopped and hissed at him. 'You don't know the difference between friends and food.'

Lizard was shaking with rage. 'I told you he was my friend. I said—and you—you—' He was so upset that the words would not come out.

'It's all relative,' said Snake.

'He—he wasn't a relative. He was a frog and he was my friend!'

Snake raised her head. 'For me frogs are food! Look at you! You have little black wings stuck to your mouth! Doesn't it occur to you that the flies you gobbled were someone's friends?'

Lizard quickly brushed his mouth. 'Flies don't have friends.'

'How do you know?' demanded Snake. 'They might have very close friendships with other flies. Right now the black flies are waking up, and there will be the heart-rending sound of fly-sobbing over the ones that are missing.'

'That's ridiculous!' snapped Lizard. 'Flies don't sob!'

'Then why do you think fly rhymes with cry?' answered Snake.

'You'll say any stupid thing to pretend you're right!' As the sun grew warmer, so did their argument about the difference between friends and food. They could have argued all morning, except that Lizard, with his superior sight, spotted a buzzard circling slowly above them.

'Home!' he said. 'Hurry! It's a buzzard!'

They sped over the short distance to their burrow before the hungry buzzard could swoop.

Buzzards did not regard snakes and lizards as friends.

The Message

It was early in the day. Snake was out for a morning slither, and Lizard was thinking about his sisters and brothers. He hadn't seen any of them for a long time. How many were left? He didn't know. He supposed that by now he had hundreds of nieces and nephews. He imagined all those little lizards scuttling around squeaking, and he felt homesick.

His family lived far away, near a barn by a cornfield,

but a visit was manageable in a day. If he left now, he could be back at the burrow before the sun set. He'd have to let Snake know. His friend would be worried if she came back and found him missing. But where had Snake gone? She'd told him when he was half asleep, and he'd forgotten.

He was greatly relieved to see Old Porcupine plodding past the burrow. Lizard ran out and put his face close to the porcupine's nose. 'Old Porcupine! I'm really, really glad to see you. Snake will be home soon. Can you give her a message? Please tell her I'm going to see my family and I'll be back before dark. Will you do that?'

'Oh sure,' said Old Porcupine. 'I'll tell her.'

'Thank you! Thank you!' squealed Lizard, and he ran off across the desert.

Porcupine went on his way. He didn't want to wait for Snake, and he didn't know where to look for her. When he saw Flycatcher Bird on a barrel cactus, he had an idea. Birds went up in the air. They saw things he didn't see. 'Howdy, Flycatcher,' he said. 'You seen Snake anywhere?'

Flycatcher Bird twitched her tail. 'Saw her a while ago. She's around some place.'

'Will you give her a message?' said Porcupine. 'Tell her Lizard's gone to see his cousins and his back is to the dark.'

'Okay,' twitted Flycatcher.

'It's important,' said Porcupine. 'Don't forget.'

'When I say okay, I mean okay!' said Flycatcher, stretching her wings.

She flew away, expecting to find Snake asleep under the rock that hung over the burrow, but instead of Snake she found a squirrel crouching in the shade. 'That's Snake's place,' said Flycatcher.

'I know,' said Squirrel. 'Snake is my Helper. I'm waiting for her to come back.'

'Goody-oh!' said the bird. 'Then you can give Snake an important message.

It's about Lizard. He's gone to see family and he's in the dark. Remember that?'

Squirrel nodded and said she'd remember. She repeated the message several times to herself. She would tell Snake as soon as Snake appeared.

Except that Snake did not arrive, and the squirrel

wondered if she'd gone to the wrong meeting place. Oh dear, oh dear! A situation like this was not good for a squirrel that needed help for extreme nervousness. Maybe she should go home and forget about the appointment. But what about the message? Oh shivers! She had promised.

Squirrel was greatly relieved to see Grey Rat running through the shadows.

She called to him. He paused and turned his head, eyes alert. 'What?'

'Have you seen Snake?'

Grey Rat bared his teeth. 'Why would I want to see Snake?'

'I don't know where she is,' cried Squirrel. 'Now I

need to go home. But there is a message. It's important. It's urgent. It's about Lizard.'

Grey Rat blinked. He trusted Snake about as far as he could throw a mountain. Lizard, however, was a different matter, a bit silly at times but likeable enough. 'What message?'

'Snake has to know!' cried Squirrel. 'Lizard went to see his family but now he's blind. He must have had an accident.'

A change came over Rat. His mouth opened and closed, and his eyes went soft. 'I'm very sorry to hear that. Blind? Poor Lizard!' He shook his head. 'How will he get home?'

'Will you tell Snake?'

'Of course I will,' said Rat. 'You hurry off home.'

All this time, Snake had been asleep in the shade of a Joshua tree. When she woke, she realised it was afternoon and she had probably missed an appointment with that jittery squirrel. She didn't often oversleep, and she knew that Lizard would be worried because she hadn't come home. She was slithering towards the burrow when Grey Rat appeared.

Snake stopped and raised her head. She didn't like Grey Rat. When he was in a negative mood, he could be very aggressive. Her tongue flickered and she tasted the air. No. No nasty mood. She actually sensed sympathy and kindness. From a rat? Surely not!

'What is it?' she demanded.

'I'm sorry. I've got bad news,' said Rat. 'It's about Lizard. He can't see his family because he's had an accident and he's blind.'

'No!'

'I'm afraid it's true. I promised a squirrel I'd pass on the message.'

Snake shook from head to tail. 'No, no, no!' was all she could say, as if that word would make it go away. 'It can't be true! Not my friend Lizard!'

'I'm sorry!' Rat didn't know what to say. 'You and Lizard have helped so many of us—'

'Where is he?' hissed Snake. 'I have to go to him.'

'I don't know.' Rat stepped back because Snake was becoming very agitated. 'You'd have to ask that squirrel. She was waiting for you. I think she knows.'

'Where is he? Where is he?' Snake swayed from side

to side, her eyes wide and wild. 'I have to be with him! Tell me!'

Her loss of control was too much for the rat. He turned and ran.

Snake was helpless with grief. All she could think of was the miserable way she had treated her dear friend Lizard. The names she had called him! The times she'd told him he was stupid! Her trick of putting her name first on their Helping sign!

Today she had been sleeping while this kind, gentle, warm-hearted idiot had been in an accident that had made him blind. She cried out loud, 'How could this happen?'

'How could what happen?' squeaked a small voice.

There, by her side was Lizard.

Snake gulped. 'You!' She flung herself at him, touching his face with her tongue. 'Your eyes! You can see!'

Lizard snorted. 'I can see you're in a right old state. Are you okay?'

'What was the accident? Did a tree fall on you?'

'Didn't Old Porcupine give you my message?'

'No, not Old Porcupine. It was Grey Rat.' Snake relaxed a little. 'You mean you didn't have an accident?'

Lizard looked concerned. 'No. Oh Snake, you're talking nonsense. Did you eat a poisonous toad?'

Now Snake was feeling that she had been the victim of some horrible hoax. She slid back a little and said, 'What was your message?'

'It was simple,' said Lizard. 'I told Old Porcupine I

was going to see my family and I would be back before dark.'

'Was that all?' said Snake,

'Yes.'

'But what about being blind?'

'No! Snake, what are you talking about? You've become very strange.'

Snake wanted to say she was not strange, just confused, and now, in spite of her long sleep, she was very tired. It was time to go back to the burrow. Tomorrow she would get to the bottom of the mystery, and pity help the animal that had made up lies to torment her.

Lizard followed her. 'Don't you want to hear about my day?'

'No!' hissed Snake. 'I've heard enough about it already.'

A Very Strange Habit

They were told the amazing story by a ring-necked dove who vowed it was true. Human things burnt their food before they ate it.

'Do you believe that?' Lizard asked Snake.

Snake considered the question. 'Doves are usually reliable. They visit the dens of human things, and they have good eyes.'

Lizard scratched his head. 'I don't think it's true. I once

saw a human she-thing eat watermelon. She cut it in bits and put it straight into her mouth. No fire.'

'Maybe they can't burn watermelon because it has water.'

'Then what food do they burn?'

Snake thought for a long time. 'I should have asked Ring-Necked Dove. She said they made a fire outside their house and burnt food in it. But she didn't say what the food was.'

'Couldn't you still ask her?'

'No,' said Snake. 'It's her egg time and she's gone away. Every year she builds her nest in the same place—on top of a human thing's house.'

'Oh,' said Lizard. 'Then she must see a lot of food getting burnt. What I want to know is, what kind of food tastes so bad it has to be put in a fire?'

'We'll find out when Ring-Necked Dove comes back,' said Snake.

'That's a long wait,' grumbled Lizard. 'I may have forgotten about it by then.'

But the wait was not long. A few days later, a rabbit told them there were two human things in a skin house by the river. What's more, they'd made a fire.

Snake looked at Lizard. 'They are going to burn their food!'

Together, they withered faster than usual along the track to the river. Walk, slither, walk, slither. From a distance, they saw a yellow skin house like half a sun pegged into the dirt. Two human things sat beside it, and in front of them was a fire with flames almost invisible in the bright light.

Lizard stopped. 'Oh Snake. I think they might be burning their meal! Why else would they have a fire on a hot day?' He had a sudden, horrible thought that made him gasp. 'Snake, I've changed my mind. Let's go back!'

'But don't we want to see it?' said Snake.

Lizard quivered. 'What if they're burning a snake? Or a poor little helpless lizard?'

Realising he was afraid, Snake rested her head on him. 'Courage, my friend. I'd proceed on my own but I don't see well. You are my eyes.' She gave him a kindly nudge. 'Whatever is in that fire, it won't be us. Right?'

They crept forward through reeds, Snake slightly ahead, trying not to imagine a charred snake in the flames. Eventually they came to the edge of the clearing. Snake could see the pale-orange flame of the fire and feel its heat. Her tongue could taste charcoal in the air. But what was in the flames? She pushed Lizard until his head was out of the reeds.

Lizard gasped, then shook again from head to tail.

'What is it?' Snake asked.

'I saw it! I saw their food in the fire!' he cried.

Snake felt him quiver with laughter. 'What?' she demanded.

'Oh Snake, this is so funny! Human things eat wood!'

Memory

It was a beautiful day, not too hot, and Lizard wanted to go for a wither with Snake, a nice long walk and slither to the red hill called Mesa Roja.

For an instant, Snake was enthusiastic, but then her long body drooped. 'We can't,' she said. 'We have a client. Old Squirrel is coming for help.'

Lizard sighed. 'Old Squirrel can't be helped. When an animal is old, she can't be made young again.'

Snake agreed. 'I know, but she's sure we can help her remember things.'

'We can't!' Lizard tapped his head with a claw. 'Her memory has turned into a forgettery. There is nothing we can do. Why did you make an appointment?'

'If I had refused,' said Snake, 'she would have told everyone in the desert we wouldn't help her. What would that have done for our reputation?'

Lizard shook his head. 'She wouldn't have remembered long enough to tell everyone.' Then his face brightened. 'Maybe she'll forget she's coming to see us.'

But Old Squirrel didn't forget. A little before high sun, she turned up at their entrance, fussing and fuming, complaining that they had shifted their burrow. 'You were on that rise past the old Joshua tree.'

'That wasn't us,' said Lizard. 'You're thinking of Doctor Grey Rabbit.'

'I am not thinking of rabbits!' she snapped. 'I'm not that stupid! Well! Are you going to help me?'

Snake slid to one side of the entrance. 'Certainly. Please come into our new reception room.'

Squirrel was very old. Her face fur was grey and she walked as though her bones were broken sticks. Lizard felt a rush of kindness. He whispered to Snake, 'Poor old thing. We'll probably be like her one day.'

'Speak for yourself!' hissed Snake.

In the reception room, Old Squirrel sat back on her haunches and peered around her. 'New, eh? I told you you'd shifted your burrow. You can't fool me.'

Lizard was about to explain when Snake took over. 'How may we help you, Mrs Squirrel?' she said in a very professional voice.

She stared at her. 'Don't you know?'

'You told me you're forgetful,' Snake continued. 'What kind of thing do you forget?'

The squirrel twitched with irritation. 'If I could remember, I wouldn't be here!'

Lizard tried. 'Dear Squirrel, do you know why you forget? It's because you've lived a long time. You have too many memories in your head, and they're squashing each other. So some memories get turned into forgetteries.' He waved his paws, pleased at his clever diagnosis. 'You shouldn't worry. It happens to all creatures who have had long and fascinating lives.'

'What happens?' she said.

'Forgetfulness,' said Snake.

Old Squirrel glared. 'What have I forgotten now?'

It seemed that nothing they said made sense to her.

Snake suggested she make marks in the dirt to remind her of things. Squirrel wanted to know why Snake thought there was dirt in her tree. Lizard asked her if she had children who could help her to remember. Yes, she did have children but she had forgotten who they were. This kind of useless talk went on until late afternoon.

Finally, Old Squirrel stood on four feet and shook her tail. She actually smiled at them. 'Have to go now. Thank you. I feel much better. You are very good Helpers.'

As she hobbled to the entrance, Lizard made a small squeak. 'Excuse me, Mrs Squirrel. There's a small matter. The payment!'

'Consultation fee,' called Snake. 'That will cost you one egg.'

Old Squirrel stopped and turned. 'An egg? Are you mad?'

'It's most reasonable.' Snake's voice was sterner. 'For the time you've been here, it should be three eggs, but we're giving you a special discount—'

'Squirrels don't lay eggs!' she yelled.

'Please,' said Lizard. 'It's payment. We know you don't lay eggs—'

'You call yourselves Helpers and you don't know the difference between a squirrel and a duck!'

Lizard could take no more of this unproductive talk. 'Forget it!' he yelled. 'Just forget it!'

Old Squirrel showed her teeth, made a humphing noise and, without another word, went out.

'What a waste of time!' said Lizard.

'No,' Snake said calmly. 'The time wasn't wasted. She needed someone to talk to, and we were it. We helped her, Lizard.'

But at that moment, Old Squirrel came limping back. She pushed her face close to Lizard's. 'Forget what?' she demanded.

What Is a River?

The next morning, Snake and Lizard, Helper and Helper, put a CLOSED notice at their entrance and set out for the red hill. The safest path to Mesa Roja was through an area of desert plants that hid small creatures from buzzards and hawks. Not that all plants were comfortable companions. The spiky agave and yucca didn't offer friendly shelter, and the prickly pear cactus was about as welcoming as a grumpy porcupine. Still, the undergrowth was a good defence, especially against hungry birds. Apart from a quick scurry to hide from a red-tailed hawk, they had an uneventful journey.

When they reached the rocky foothills of Mesa Roja, they found many cracks and hollows where they could hide from buzzards.

The hill itself was not very high and was flat on top so Lizard could see all around him. For Snake, the view was blurred like something spilt or squashed, so Lizard needed to point out familiar features. 'Over there is the rabbit colony. Behind it, far away, is the River of Death.' He pointed to the road. 'There are three monsters on it, running fast, one blue and two black. The sun is glinting on their eyes. Can you see them, Snake?'

'No,' said Snake. 'Go on—what else?'

Lizard turned and stretched a front leg. 'Can you see the mountains?'

'I can see you better,' Snake replied. 'What's wrong with your foot? Cramp? Cactus thorn?'

'I'm pointing at the mountains! Oh Snake, turn your head a little. Surely you can see huge, enormous mountains!'

Snake's eyes were not made for long-distance viewing, but there was something long and dark in front of her. 'Like cloud fallen down?'

'Yes, yes! That's it!' Lizard was excited. 'Now, over this way, you can look at the river.'

Snake turned and saw only a blur of brown and orange. 'A river is smaller than a mountain,' she said.

Lizard's arm went up and down like a branch in a wind. 'Down there! Try, Snake. Concentrate! There's not much water but you can see it—curving across the desert in big loops. Look! There's our swampy patch of reeds!'

Snake could not see it. She put her head on the ground and closed her eyes, pretending she wasn't interested. 'The river has curves because it was made by my ancestor the great Sky Serpent. She made all rivers. She thought the land looked dry, so she came down and slithered through it. She made long, deep channels. If it wasn't for my ancestor, there would be no rivers.'

Lizard dropped down beside Snake. 'That's interesting. Did you know it was my ancestor the great Sky Dragon who filled the rivers with water?'

'How?'

He thought for a moment. 'She filled her mouth with water from the clouds.' Then he added, 'She had a very big mouth.'

Snake opened one eye. She wanted to say, so that's why lizards have big mouths, but she knew he didn't like lizard jokes. Instead she said, 'We've seen everything. It's time we withered back home.'

As they started on the downward slope, Lizard said, 'A river can't be a river if there's no water in it.'

'Yes it can,' said Snake.

'No it can't.'

'My ancestor made that channel!' Snake made a curved track in the dust to demonstrate river-making. 'The channel had to come first. Otherwise, the water would have run everywhere and been wasted.'

'It's not the channel that holds the water in.' Lizard's voice became shrill. 'It's the banks!'

'The banks are part of the channel.'

74

'No, they're not!'

'Yes, they are! My ancestor the great Sky Serpent made the banks as well!'

Lizard squeaked, 'That's nonsense! When snakes wriggle they make loops in the sand, but they don't make banks to hold the loops in place. Someone else must have made the banks.'

Snake slid ahead. She turned a little and called, 'You talk too much!'

It was unfair, and she knew it. Lizard became very quiet, and for a while neither of them spoke. The track back to the burrow seemed much longer than it had been that morning, and they were both tired and hungry when they reached home.

Snake knew she had to break the silence. 'That was a very interesting wither.'

'Yes, it was,' murmured Lizard. After a long pause, he said, 'I'm glad you saw the mountains.'

'So am I.' Snake slid to their egg store and selected a fresh duck egg. 'I prefer mountains to rivers. The problem with a river is it keeps changing. Actually, you never really know what a river is. Is it the water?

Is it the earth under the water? Is it the banks?' She turned to Lizard. 'Would you like an egg?'

'Yes, please!' Lizard found a sparrow egg. 'You are right, dear Snake. Mountains are much more reliable.'

The Aunts

Lizard had hundreds of relatives who hardly ever paid him a visit. The reason, of course, was Snake, who had a large mouth and a tongue that flickered when she saw them. All of Lizard's aunts were greatly surprised that the couple were still Lizard and Snake, and not Lizard in Snake.

As time passed it became clear to the aunts that Snake and Lizard got on well together. Not only was their

Helping business most successful, it was said they had more food than they could eat themselves, mounds of dried beetles, moths, blue flies, caterpillars and quails' eggs. Nephew Lizard was very rich.

So when Aunt Forty-Nine and Aunt Twenty-Three met Lizard crossing the dry gulch by the old Joshua tree, they stopped him for a casual family talk—although they mainly talked about Snake. 'Is she difficult to live with?' asked Aunt Forty-Nine.

Lizard, who was in a happy mood, answered, 'She is my very, very, very best friend.'

Aunt Forty-Nine wagged a claw at him. 'But I'll bet you have to watch your back.'

That puzzled Lizard. 'I can't watch my back. It's behind me.'

Aunt Twenty-Three said, 'What we mean is—how careful are you? Everyone knows her sort eats lizards.'

'No, no!' Now he was shocked. 'Snake would never eat a lizard, cross my heart and hope to die. She eats eggs, maybe a frog or two, but she doesn't touch lizards. Absolutely not! She has a vow.'

'Vow? That's some sort of diet?' asked Aunt Twenty-Three.

'No, it's a very serious promise that she will not eat a lizard in her whole, entire, existing life.'

Aunts Forty-Nine and Twenty-Three exchanged smiles, and Forty-Nine said, 'Thank you, dear nephew. That's good news indeed. We are very pleased to hear it.'

That's how it all began. Soon after, a noisy group of fifteen lizard aunts called to see Snake and Lizard.

It was the first time there had been a friendly visit from Lizard's family, and the Helpers gave them an enthusiastic welcome. This was a historic occasion, and they celebrated it with great hospitality. By the time the aunts had finished heaps of delicious blue flies, sun-dried beetles and cactus worms, they were too tired to go home. Snake kindly told them they could sleep in the new consulting room near the entrance of the burrow.

The next morning, the fifteen aunts were still there.

Snake slithered past their chatter to find Lizard outside in a patch of sunlight. 'I thought I'd find you here,' she said. 'Nice party, wasn't it?'

Lizard nodded and waited for the question.

'When are they going home?' murmured Snake.

'Soon,' said Lizard. 'Very soon. I hope.'

'They don't seem in any hurry,' said Snake. 'We have clients coming this morning.'

Lizard looked a little twitchy. 'They all have homes to go to. But perhaps they'll want breakfast first.'

'After that meal last night? Oh Lizard! Your pantry is nearly bare!'

'We still have some sparrow's eggs,' said Lizard.

Snake's mood changed. 'Those are my eggs!' she hissed.

'Mine? Yours? What does it matter? We're Helpers, Snake. We work together to offer H-E-L-P. If you had your family staying the night, I would gladly give them breakfast.'

Snake wanted to say that she had no family, and if she had, then Lizard would be their breakfast, but she remembered the long discussions they'd had about what it meant to be Helpers. Reluctantly, she gave Lizard's aunts a sparrow-egg breakfast.

The aunts were full of praise for their generosity. Aunt

Forty-Nine stood on her hind legs to make a speech. 'Never have we had such an extraordinary welcome. Nephew, there was a time when we thought you wouldn't amount to much, but now your reputation as a Helper is known throughout the desert. Dear Snake, your reputation for kindness not only covers the desert, it also reaches to the skies. For that reason, Snake, we now make you an honorary member of all lizard tribes.'

She spoke with such emotion that the other lizard aunts squeaked and clicked a chorus of cheers that embarrassed both Snake and Lizard. Snake didn't know how to respond, so Lizard stood tall and shouted, 'Thank you! Thank you, Aunts. But now this must end. We have clients coming this morning and we need our consulting room.'

A silence fell like a blanket over the aunts and they looked at each other. Then they all started muttering. Number Forty-Nine stamped her hind feet for attention. 'Of course we must leave your consulting room. Isn't that so?' She turned to the others, who looked doubtful. She then smiled at Snake and Lizard.

'By the labour of your scales, you made that room for your clients, and by the labour of our scales, we can dig a room for ourselves. Come, girls! Never let it be said that we were scared of hard work.' Head held high, she marched to the back of the burrow, followed by the other aunts.

This happened so quickly, it was a while before Snake understood what the aunts intended. 'They're going to stay!' she hissed at Lizard. 'They mean to live here. Do something!'

'S-s-such as?' stammered Lizard.

'They're your family. Tell them they have to leave! Now!'

Lizard was shaking. 'I can't. Oh Snake, it's the rule of family. No lizard can ever turn away another lizard.'

Snake stretched to full length as a chorus of squeaks and a small cloud of dust came out of the darkness. 'So we just let fifteen lizards move in with us and eat all our food?'

'There'll be m-m-more than f-f-fifteen when the news g-gets out,' cried Lizard.

'I'll evict them,' hissed Snake. 'I don't have any silly family rule!'

'Y-y-yes you do! That's why they made you an honorary l-l-l-lizard.'

'What?'

But by now Lizard was crying and couldn't speak.

'Wait here,' hissed Snake. 'I'll tell them the party's definitely over!'

With her head and upper body raised, her tongue tasting the dark, dust-filled air, she slid down the U-shaped burrow to the bend where fifteen lizards were scratching chunks of dirt from the back wall. She couldn't get close, nor could her hisses be heard. The only way to get attention was to nudge one of those stupid aunts.

That worked. The squeak was so loud, it silenced the others and Snake could speak.

'Stop this at once! You are not moving into our burrow.'

Aunt Forty-Nine pushed through the group and stood in front of Snake. 'Let me tell you the lizard's family rule ...'

'I know it,' said Snake. 'But it doesn't apply to me. I'm telling you to sssscram! Sssskedaddle!'

In the darkness, there was a starlike gleam in the eyes of Aunt Forty-Nine. 'Snake, you are now an honorary member of the lizard tribe, so it does apply to you. We like it here and we intend to stay. You can hiss all you like. We're not afraid.' Aunt Forty-Nine came closer. 'We happen to know you have a vow.'

There was a buzz of clicks and squeaks from the other aunts, and some of them went back to scratching at the dirt wall. Snake turned and slid up the burrow to where Lizard was waiting, his claws twitching like fly's legs.

'Go away,' Snake said. 'Go on! Go for a wither.'

'What about—?'

'I'm going to chase your aunts out of our home,' said Snake, 'and I may use language that is far from polite. You should not be here. Go! Did you hear me? Wither off!'

Lizard was only too pleased to scramble out into the clean fresh air. Still quivering, he climbed onto the rock above the burrow and waited. It was not a long wait. In fact, it was very short. Like a seed bursting out of a pod, Aunt Twenty-Three popped out of the entrance. Lizard called goodbye but she didn't hear him. As she ran across the desert, another aunt came out, then another and another. Lizard counted them. Twelve, thirteen, fourteen. They scampered in a line as though a fox were after them.

Lizard waited for the last aunt, but no one else came out, and everything was so still that even the sun seemed stuck in the sky. A funny feeling came into his stomach as he crawled down the rock and into the burrow.

'Snake dear,' he called. 'Are you all right?'

Snake's voice came back from the darkness. 'I chased them out, Lizard. Don't worry. They won't come back.' There was a pause, and Snake said, 'It was hard work, Lizard, and I'm tired. I'd like to go back to sleep. Please, dear friend, do you mind taking care of our clients this morning?'

'Yes, yes, certainly. You get some rest.' Lizard swallowed. 'Snake? I counted them as they came out—fourteen aunts.'

'Fifteen,' said Snake.

'No. Aunt Forty-Nine didn't come out.'

Snake gave a warm, hissy laugh. 'Lizard, my dear, you were never good at counting.'

Lizard thought for a moment, then went into the consulting room to tidy it for the clients due mid-morning. He still had that funny ache in his stomach, but he didn't know if it was a bad feeling or a good feeling. It was hard to tell. He swept the floor and put down fresh leaves for the clients. Snake was right. He wasn't good at counting.

Helper and Helper Need Help

It could have been the heat, or it could have been the dry desert wind that blew dead leaves into their reception room. It may even have been caused by the disappearance of Aunt Forty-Nine. Whatever the reason, Snake and Lizard were irritable and could not agree on anything. If Snake wanted to go out, Lizard wanted to stay home, and if Lizard was in a talking mood, Snake went to sleep.

Snake looked at the yellow sunset. 'Wind again tomorrow.'

'No,' said Lizard. 'Tomorrow will be calm, not a puff of breeze.'

The next day, when the wind blew dust in their faces, Snake said, 'I told you so.'

'You think you know everything,' snapped Lizard.

'No,' said Snake. 'I think you know nothing.'

They'd always had discussions that came close to arguments, and at times the word play had been fun. But now disagreement had become disagreeable and the constant bickering was making them tired and edgy.

'I think we need help,' said Lizard.

'No,' said Snake. 'We give help. We don't ask for it.'

Lizard thought of the time when they had been such good neighbours they had dug out the wall between their burrows. He sniffed. 'Maybe we should put back the wall—make two burrows again.'

'Definitely not,' said Snake. 'The solution is very simple—you have to stop being a grouch!'

'I'm not a grouch!' screeched Lizard. 'But I live with one!'

They were both unhappy, and each blamed the other. Eventually, Snake suggested that they visit Wise Tortoise, who lived near the desert in the human thing's watermelon patch.

'You said we didn't need help,' said Lizard.

'We don't!' hissed Snake. 'We need advice. Wise Tortoise is nearly a hundred years old and she knows everything. She'll tell us who's at fault.'

They left the next morning on a long wither to a small farm near the road they called the River of Death. The farm had rain that came out of pipes in the ground, so everything was green, including a cornfield and a patch of watermelon vines. Unfortunately, neither the corn nor the watermelons were ripe, but because the farm was small, they had no trouble finding Wise Tortoise under the melon leaves. She was indeed ancient and slow, but her eyes in their nets of wrinkles were very sharp.

'What's the problem?' she asked.

At once, Snake and Lizard began blaming each other, shouting to drown the other's voice.

'He argues with everything!' cried Snake.

'She's totally unreasonable!' screeched Lizard.

Wise Tortoise listened for a while, then said, 'Stop! Stop! Stop!'

They closed their mouths.

'What do you want of me?' said Tortoise.

Lizard yelled, 'She says it's me! It isn't! It's her!'

Snake uncoiled and smiled at Wise Tortoise. 'You see how he loses control? He's impossible to live with. The plain fact is, he won't agree on anything. We are here because you are a creature of great age and understanding. You will know who's the cause of this unpleasant situation. Tell us who's at fault.'

The old tortoise nodded slowly. 'Wait while I consider the facts.' Then she drew her head into her shell until her face was completely hidden.

Snake and Lizard waited. The earth was dark and damp, but the wind was still dry. It rustled the leaves over their heads, and the dancing shadows made Tortoise look as though she was moving. In fact, she was so still they couldn't see if she were even breathing. They waited and waited. Some of the vines near them had yellow flowers curling back over the beginnings of melons. Further away was a melon half-formed, like a pale-green stone.

'I think she's gone to sleep,' whispered Lizard.

'Of course she hasn't gone to sleep,' said Snake.

After another long wait, there was a small movement and the head of the tortoise slowly emerged from the shell. Her dark eyes turned to Snake and Lizard. 'I have an answer for you,' she said.

'Yes?' They leaned forward.

Wise Tortoise cleared her throat. 'When two creatures quarrel, both are in the wrong.' Then her head disappeared again.

She hadn't asked for a consultation fee, and just as well, because they would have refused to pay her. They hurried through the watermelon vines, unable to believe they had come so far for so little.

'We would never treat our clients like that,' said Snake.

'Never!' said Lizard. 'She might be old but she certainly isn't wise.'

'The most unwise tortoise I've met!' said Snake.

'Utterly and absolutely!' Lizard was stopped by a sudden thought. 'Oh Snake! We both agreed!'

Snake nodded. 'Of course we did! There can be no argument about that tortoise. Why did we ask advice of someone less wise than ourselves?'

As they came out of the watermelon patch, the afternoon wind blew dust in their faces. Snake looked at Lizard. 'It might be calm tomorrow.'

'Yes, it might,' said Lizard.

Silence

Friends again, Snake and Lizard decided that from now on they would solve their own problems. Life had become much more agreeable, but little differences still existed, and after an entire morning of listening to Lizard chatter, Snake needed to say something. 'Lizard, dear, I hope you won't be offended. There is something we must discuss.'

Lizard smiled. 'Of course I won't be offended. Haven't we left all that nonsense behind, dear Snake? We have come to a place of great trust in our friendship, and you know that you can—'

'You talk too much,' said Snake.

'What?'

'I said, you talk too much. You go on and on about silly things.'

'Like what?'

'Like the number of flies you eat for breakfast. Green. Blue. One fly with three legs. Plus I get every detail of your ninety-eight brothers and sisters. It's so boring!'

Lizard was offended. 'Just because you were one lonely and only egg, that doesn't give you the right to—to criticise!' His voice became high-pitched. 'You are so self-centred, Snake!'

'Quiet!' hissed Snake. 'This isn't going to be one of our old arguments. Lizard, please! I'm not criticising you. I'm simply saying there are times when I value a little silence.'

Lizard's face went stiff. 'You want silence? Good. I'll stop talking. I won't talk again for three full moons.'

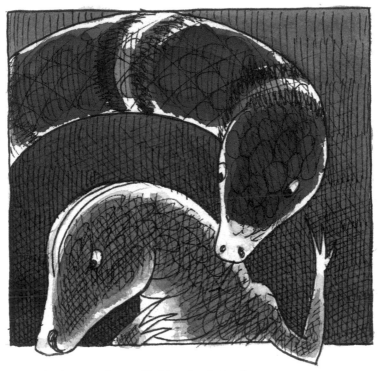

'Isn't that rather silly?' asked Snake.

Lizard's mouth was a tight, thin line.

'Do you actually mean it?' Snake asked.

Lizard gave her a small, firm nod.

'How will you communicate?' said Snake. 'You are a Helper. You have to talk to your clients.'

Lizard turned his head away.

Snake tried to be reasonable. 'Let's discuss this. If you don't want to speak to me for three moons, I accept that. But we have to talk now, to put strategies in place. How do you plan to manage this silence? I need to know.'

Still, Lizard would not speak.

Snake put her head closer to Lizard's and saw uncertainty flickering in his eyes. 'My dear friend, start your silence tomorrow. That will give us both some time to plan it.'

At first, Lizard allowed himself only a few words, but before long he was offering some useful ideas about other forms of communication. He would still talk to clients, but on his own. To Snake, he would make signals—a twitch in each leg, counting on claws, a flick of the tail up or down, head nods and shakes.

The signals were complicated, and Snake hoped they would remember their meanings.

Lizard reassured her. 'You'll get used to them. Silent signals can be better than talk. For example, if a coyote sneaked up on you, I would signal a warning. No noise!'

'That would help you,' said Snake. 'You wouldn't be drawing attention to yourself. But how would it help me?'

'Okay. Look at it the other way. The coyote is behind me, and you send a signal.'

'I'd give a loud hiss,' said Snake. 'I'd try to make it sound venomous.'

Lizard smiled in a patient way. 'You're teasing. I know you think my ideas won't work. But they will, Snake, and you'll have weeks and weeks of your beautiful quiet.'

Snake felt weary. Lizard had talked more about his plans for silence than he'd talked about green and blue flies. But when day ended, she was touched by Lizard's goodnight speech. 'Snake, my very dear friend, I will be in silence tomorrow. Therefore, I want you to remember my last words for three full moons. Here they are. You are the best friend I ever had.' Then he closed his eyes.

She didn't go to sleep for a long time. She felt that someone had drawn a line through her long body. One half of her was longing for restful silence. The other half was already missing his prattle.

It was late when she woke up. Lizard was rolling two eggs into the burrow and shouting, 'Breakfast! Breakfast! Great find! Two fresh roadrunner eggs!'

Snake uncoiled. 'Wh-what?'

'There were four in the nest. I thought they wouldn't miss two, and if they did, they could lay some more. I know how much you love these eggs!'

Snake blinked. 'Lizard, you said you would begin your silence tomorrow.'

Lizard shrugged. 'Oh Snake, dear! This isn't tomorrow. This is today!'

Simple Addition

Snake didn't like toads. Lizard thought it was because Snake had once made a mistake and swallowed one. The disagreeable stuff on the toad's skin had made Snake ill for days. Not that she'd admit the reason for her dislike. 'Toads are so bad-mannered,' she hissed. 'They are beyond help.'

Lizard explained. 'These three toads have travelled all night. They don't need help. All they want is a cool, dark place to rest during the day. They'll be off again at sunset.' Lizard cleared his throat. 'I—ah—said they could use our reception room.'

Snake raised her head. 'You what?'

'Only for a day. There's no one else, no appointments. Snake, it wouldn't hurt to have three guests for—'

'You know how I feel about toads!' Snake hissed.

'Ten quail eggs,' Lizard said quickly.

Snake's mouth closed. She leaned close and said, 'They're paying?'

'Ten eggs in advance,' said Lizard.

Snake could not believe it. 'Fresh?' she asked.

'Very fresh,' said Lizard. 'Is your answer yes?'

Of course it was yes. Never before had there been such a handsome payment.

The three guests were she-toads with large eyes and poisonous warts on their backs. Snake held back a shudder and told herself that if she were a he-toad she might find these three handsome. But that didn't erase the memory of a huge stomach-ache.

As Snake helped Lizard stack eggs at the back of the burrow, she tried to fill her mind with kind thoughts.

She was a Helper, and Helpers must believe good things about other creatures. 'They are very generous toads,' she said.

'Too generous,' said Lizard. 'Snake, I think we have too many eggs. Look at them all!'

Their egg store was indeed large. Adding ten quail eggs to it made it excessive. Snake searched for another kind thought. 'We could give them a refund,' she said.

Lizard nodded. 'What do you suggest?'

'Half,' said Snake, now very pleased with her thinking. 'Lizard, give them back five eggs. Do it now before they settle down to sleep.'

It was much easier to roll eggs down the burrow than to roll them back up. Lizard found it difficult to manage five quail eggs, and halfway up the tunnel, he stopped for a rest. A refund of five eggs for three toads? Lizard wasn't clever with numbers, but even he knew that five didn't share equally with three. It would save a lot of bother if he ate two eggs. So that's what he did. In a dark corner of the burrow, he broke open the shells of two eggs and sucked out the sweet, fresh yolk. He then swept the crushed shells

to one side and continued to roll three eggs up to the reception room.

He gave each of the three sleepy toads an egg. They were very grateful for the refund. 'Thank you, Lizard!' said one. 'You and Snake are very kind. This means we've paid only seven eggs for your cosy room.'

Lizard went back down the burrow, deep in thought. Originally, the toads had paid ten eggs. Then they had received a refund of one egg each. Three eggs! That meant they had now paid seven eggs. And on the way, Lizard had eaten two eggs.

Lizard counted on his claws. Seven and two made nine. He knew that was right. Seven plus two had to make nine. But they had paid ten. So where was the other egg?

The problem worried him so much that his head hurt, but he could not possibly go to Snake for an answer.

A Silly Idea

Bull Frog arrived out of breath because he'd been hurrying. This was not due to any danger but because he had a question that would not let him rest. He had barely reached the reception room, when out it came in a grunt. 'Is Earth flat?'

'Yes!' said Snake.

'Of course it's flat,' said Lizard.

Bull Frog's bulging eyes held doubt. 'Wise Tortoise

says Earth is round like the moon and the sun.'

Lizard thought about that. 'It's possible you're both right. Earth could be round and flat.'

The bull frog grunted. 'Wise Tortoise said round like a ball.'

Snake smiled at him. 'How did you come here?'

'I walked.' He was still puffing. 'Rather fast.'

'Did you find Earth flat? Or did you think it was round like a ball? Were you leaning sideways, afraid you would fall off?'

'What do you mean?' asked Bull Frog.

'What Snake means,' said Lizard, 'is that the Earth is definitely flat. It has to be flat for creatures to walk on it.'

'Not all of it,' said Bull Frog. 'Not mountains.'

'That is very true,' said Snake. 'A mountain is not flat, it is up-and-down. But the Earth also has holes that are down-and-up. If you put an up-and-down with a down-and-up, they cancel each other and you get flat. Do you agree?'

The frog nodded.

'Good,' said Snake. 'And don't believe anything that silly old tortoise tells you. One egg, please.'

A Fishy Story

Only one part of the river still had flowing water. It was therefore crowded with fish that in turn attracted hungry birds. Lizard was on the bank catching blue flies, while near him a heron slowly waded, eyes intent on the surface. Suddenly, the heron's long bill plunged into the water and came up with a fish. The heron then spread his wings and flew into the air,

the wriggling fish in his mouth. Two other herons took off after him. There was a scuffle in the air, some angry squawks and—plop!

The fish landed on the river bank in front of Lizard.

It was a beautiful fish! While it was too big for Lizard's mouth, he knew Snake would greatly enjoy it. He gripped the end of the fish's tail firmly between his teeth and dragged it through the reeds. Above him, the herons still fought over something they no longer possessed.

Snake did indeed love the fish. 'Oh, my dear Lizard! Do you know how rare it is for a snake to get a fish feast? This is perfect! Look at that plump body! Look at those silver scales!'

Snake's gratitude greatly pleased Lizard. He watched while she delicately opened her jaws to fit around the fish's head, and he felt more pleasure to see the way her eyes closed in bliss as the fish slid into her mouth. 'Superb!' she murmured.

Afterwards, Lizard went back to the river for more flies. He wasn't keen to meet the heron, so he went to one of the muddy swamps further away. He was still very pleased with himself.

The heron, however, was feeling no pleasure whatsoever. He had seen his fish drop in front of that silly little lizard that ran around minding everyone else's business. By the time the bird had got rid of his greedy relatives, the lizard and fish had gone.

Heron worked it out. The fish was too big for Lizard to swallow, so he must have dragged it back to his lair. Yes, indeed! The heron spread his wings and flew in a straight line towards the sign: SNAKE AND LIZARD, HELPER AND HELPER.

Snake, whose stomach was pleasantly full, had been half-expecting the visit. She coiled her body so that her tail was over the bulge, and when Heron poked his beak into the entrance, she gave him a cheerful 'Good morning!'

'Where is he?' snapped Heron.

'You mean Lizard the Helper?' she asked.

'I mean Lizard the thief! He took my fish! You can't deny it, because I saw him.'

Snake smiled and nodded. 'Of course he took your fish. He's a Helper and he helped it. He put it back in the river.'

'He what?'

'Put it in the water,' Snake said patiently. 'He felt sorry for the poor little thing.'

Heron let out a series of angry shrieks and pulled his head out of the burrow.

'He had terrible manners,' Snake said when Lizard came back. 'I couldn't repeat the things he said about you. You would be very upset.'

Lizard felt uncomfortable. 'Well, you did tell him a lie.'

'No, dear Lizard, I told him a story.'

'What's the difference?' asked Lizard. 'You said I put the fish back in the river. That's not real.'

'Yes, it is.' Snake uncoiled, stretched and yawned. 'Lizard, there is something you should know about stories. They are real. They're just a different kind of real.'